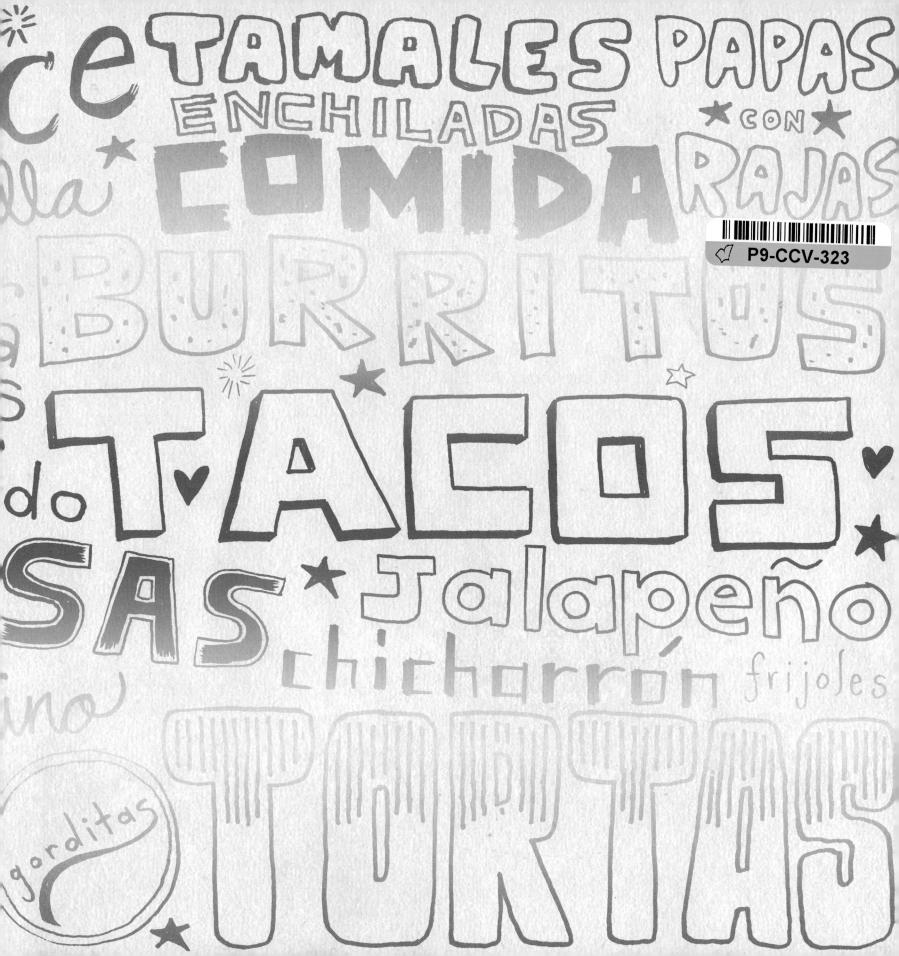

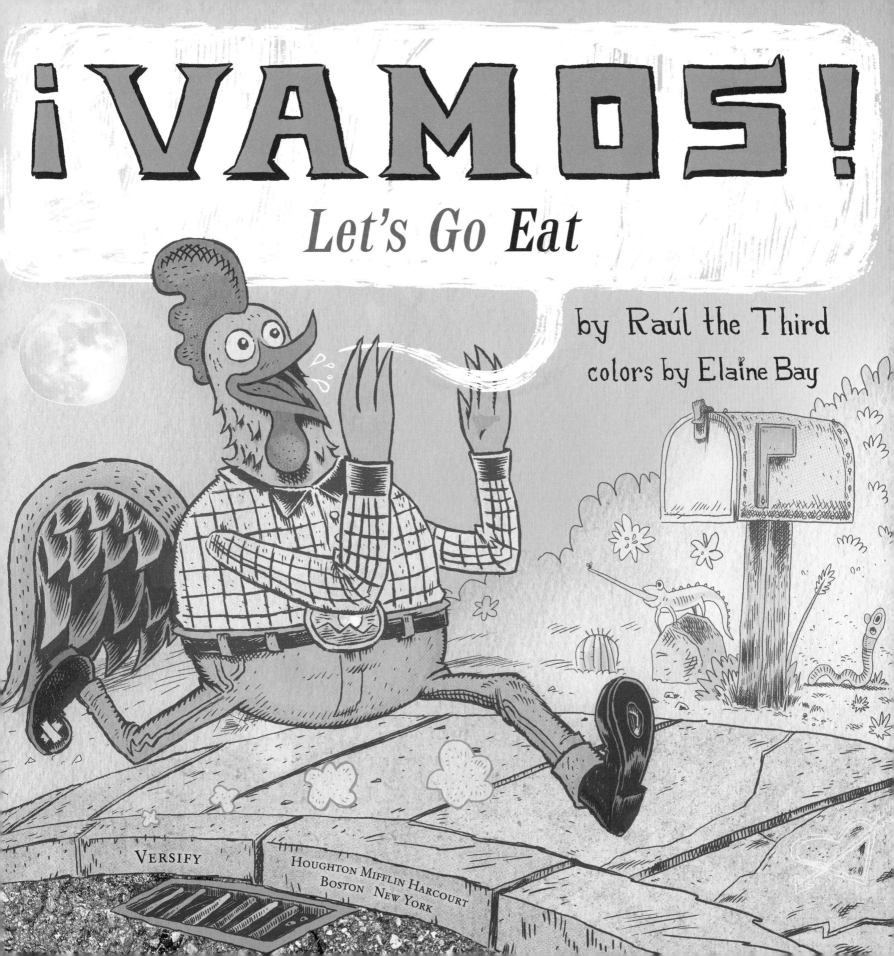

To mi mamá, Olga Moreno Gonzalez, for fresh tortillas in the morning with melted butter. She will always be my favorite person to visit for authentic Mexican food.
—Raúl

To my parents for making the journey from Canada to the border town of El Paso, where I grew up eating amazing Mexican cuisine and Hatch chile.
—Elaine

Versify is an imprint of Houghton Mifflin Harcourt Publishing Company.

hmhbooks.com

The illustrations in this book were done in ink on smooth plate
Bristol board with Adobe Photoshop for color.
The text type was set in Stempel Garamond LT Std.
The display type was set in Latin MT Std.
Hand lettering by Raúl Gonzalez

Library of Congress Cataloging-in-Publication Data
Names: Gonzalez, Raul, 1976– author, illustrator. | Bay, Elaine, 1976– colorist.
Title: ¡Vamos! Let's go eat! / by Raul the Third ; colors by Elaine Bay.
Other titles: Let's go eat | Vamos! Let us go eat
Description: Boston ; New York : Houghton Mifflin Harcourt, [2020] | Spanish words and phrases are used throughout English text. | Summary: Little Lobo, a Mexican American, and Bernabâe, his dog, gather tacos, frutas picadas, cuernos, and more and deliver them to los luchadores preparing for Lucha Libre 5000.
Identifiers: LCCN 2019008792 | ISBN 9781328557049 (paper over board)
Subjects: | CYAC: Delivery of goods—Fiction. | Food trucks—Fiction. | Wrestling—Fiction. | City and town life—Fiction. | Mexican Americans—Fiction. | Dogs—Fiction.
Classification: LCC PZ7.1.G65327 Vai 2019 | DDC [E]—dc23
LC record available at https://lccn.loc.gov/2019008792

Manufactured in China
SCP 10 9 8 7 6 5 4 3 2 1
4500786795

El Coliseo has been buzzing with excitement all day long. Everyone is busy preparing for the night's big event.

A parade of trucks slowly makes its way to el Coliseo!

Everyone is excited for the big show.
There is a long line of fans waiting to get in.

A food truck is a kitchen on wheels.

Food of all kinds can be prepared there.

Some food sellers use modified bikes or wagons.

The Painted Burro is a taco-making machine!

Salsa, anyone?

They are well known for their fresh salsas.

¡Ahí te va! Here you go!

Across the way, Pati uses a machete to slice tender meat off a spit. Her specialty is al pastor!

Ji-Woo Lynx makes tacos perfectly combining Mexican and Korean cuisine. Did somebody say kimchi? Little Lobo orders one of every taco from the trucks.

Kooky Dooky likes his taco with extra salsa. Watch where you squirt that, Kooky!

Next on the list is a visit to the elotero. At the elotero, the corn boils in a giant tub right on the cart.

Kooky Dooky likes to eat his right off the ground.

Macho gives all of his husks to Tammy.
She uses them to wrap her tamales.

She always gives Bernabé a sample of her masa.

Doña Chelo fills gigantic cups with aguas frescas. She uses many of the fruits and vegetables from Pato's jardín to make her juices.

Next, Little Lobo follows his nose and heads toward dessert.

The pastry cart with its hot-from-the-oven baked goods is the perfect final stop.

Finally, Little Lobo is ready to make his delivery!

Tired after a long day of making deliveries, Little Lobo buys snacks for his friends . . .

¡Cacahuates! ¡Palomitas! ¡Soda!

sits back . . .

. . . and enjoys the show!

A FOOD GLOSSARY*

*These are only some of the words found in Little Lobo's story. Be sure to look up other ones you don't know in a Spanish-English dictionary!

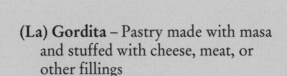

(El) Agua – Water

(El) Aguacate verde – Green avocado

(El) Ajo – Garlic

(El) Antojito – Snack food

(El) Arroz – Rice

(El) Arroz con leche – Rice with sweetened condensed milk

(El) Arroz con pollo – Chicken with rice

(El) Atole – Cornmeal-based beverage

Beber – To drink

(La) Bebida – Drink

(El) Bigote – Pastry shaped like a mustache

(El) Cacahuate – Peanut

(El) Caldo – Soup

(El) Caldo de res — Broth made with beef shank, carrots, potatoes, cabbage, and corn

(La) Canela – Cinnamon

(La) Cebolla – Onion

(El) Chicharrón – Pork rind

(Los) Chilaquiles – Fried tortilla strips simmered in red or green salsa

(El) Chile relleno – Pepper stuffed with cheese and/or meat

(La) Chilindrina – Sugar-coated bun

(La) Chirimoya – Custard apple

Comer – To eat

(La) Comida – Food

(La) Concha – Pastry with a seashell-like appearance

(El) Dulce – Sweet

(El) Flan – Custard

(El) Elote – Grilled corn on the cob

(La) Empanada – Baked or fried pastry, either savory or sweet

(Los) Esquites – Corn in a cup

(Los) Frijoles – Beans

(La) Gordita – Pastry made with masa and stuffed with cheese, meat, or other fillings

(La) Guayaba – Guava

(La) Horchata – Sweetened rice beverage

(El) Jalapeño – Hot pepper

(El) Jamón – Ham

(La) Jícama – Mexican turnip

(El) Kimchi – Korean fermented and salted vegetable condiment

(La) Lechuga – Lettuce

(El) Maíz – Corn

(El) Mantecado – Biscuit made from almonds and lard

(La) Masa – Corn dough

(El) Nopal – Prickly pear cactus

(La) Nuez – Nut

(El) Ojo de buey – Biscuit in the shape of a bull's-eye

(Las) Palomitas – Popcorn

(La) Panadería – Bakery

(Las) Papas con rajas – Potatoes mixed with poblano peppers

(El) Pastel de tres leches – Cake made from three different milks

(El) Pastelito – Little cake

(El) Pepino – Cucumber

(El) Perro caliente – Hot dog

Picoso – Spicy

(La) Piña – Pineapple

(El) Piñón – Pine nut

(El) Pollo – Chicken

(El) Pollo frito – Fried chicken

(La) Pupusa – A traditional Salvadoran dish made of a thick, handmade corn tortilla filled with queso, refried beans, and meat

(El) Queso – Cheese

(El) Raspado – Snow cone

(El) Rompope – Eggnog

(El) Sabor – Taste

Sabroso – Tasty

(La) Sandía – Watermelon

(El) Tamal – Corn dough around a filling, wrapped in corn husks or plantain leaves

(La) Torta – A kind of sandwich

(La) Tortilla – Unleavened flatbread typically made with corn or wheat

(La) Zanahoria – Carrot

(La) Zarzamora – Blackberry